Daniel Goes to the Playground

Adapted by Becky Friedman
Based on the screenplay "The Playground Is Different with Baby"
written by Jennifer Hamburg
Poses and layouts by Jason Fruchter

Simon Spotlight
New York London Toronto Sydney New Delhi

SIMON SPOTLIGHT
An imprint of Simon & Schuster Children's Publishing Division
1230 Avenue of the Americas, New York, New York 10020
This Simon Spotlight paperback edition December 2015
© 2015 The Fred Rogers Company
SIMON SPOTLIGHT and colophon are registered trademarks of Simon & Schuster, Inc.
For information about special discounts for bulk purchases, please contact Simon & Schuster
Special Sales at 1-866-506-1949 or business@simonandschuster.com.
Manufactured in the United States of America 0616 LAK
10 9 8 7 6 5 4
ISBN 978-1-4814-5198-7 (pbk)
ISBN 978-1-4814-5199-4 (eBook)

It was a beautiful day in the neighborhood, and Daniel and his family were at the playground with Prince Wednesday and Miss Elaina.

"Hi, neighbor!" said Daniel. "Margaret and I are swinging. One day she'll be big enough to go on a big kid swing like me! Right, Margaret?"

"Dan-Dan!" said Baby Margaret as she watched Daniel.

After swinging, Daniel and his friends decided to play circus. Daniel's mom and dad sat down nearby to watch the show with Baby Margaret.

First, Prince Wednesday swung on the flying trapeze.

Next, Miss Elaina walked the tightrope forward . . .

. . . and backward!

Then it was Daniel's turn.
Daniel was going to juggle.

"And now, Daniel Tiger the Grr-ific will do his tiger-tastic juggling act!" said Daniel proudly. Daniel threw one, two, three juggling balls up in the air!

"Mom! Dad! Look at me!" Daniel exclaimed as he tried to catch the balls.

But Daniel's mom and dad weren't looking at Daniel. . . .
They were helping Margaret.

Daniel felt sad.

Daniel walked over to his mom and dad. "You didn't see me juggling," he said.

"I'm sorry, Daniel," said Mom Tiger. "Your sister needed us."

"But I needed you too," said Daniel. "I needed you to watch me juggle."

"I know it can be hard when we need to pay attention to Margaret," said Mom Tiger.

"It is hard," said Daniel. "It feels . . . different. Before Margaret, you used to watch me all the time."

"That's true," said Mom. "It is different with Margaret around. But *when a baby makes things different, find a way to make things fun.*"

Daniel tried to think of a way that Margaret could make things more fun. He thought and he thought, until . . .

Margaret toddled over to Daniel, rolling the juggling balls toward him.

"That gives me an idea!" Daniel exclaimed. "Baby Margaret can help me with my juggling act, and then everyone can watch *both* of us! That will be lots of fun."

"Ga, ga, ga," said Margaret.

"Presenting Daniel the Grr-ific and his sister, and juggling helper, Margaret the Magnificent!" announced Daniel.

Daniel tossed a ball to Margaret, and Margaret rolled it back to him. They were juggling *together*! And this time, everyone was watching.

Playing circus on the playground was so much fun, Daniel made-believe that he was performing in a real circus.

"It's time for the circus parade!" announced Miss Elaina after Daniel and Margaret had finished their act. "Everyone, line up!"

Daniel, Prince Wednesday, and Miss Elaina all got in a line.

Margaret got in line too.
"No-no, Margaret, this parade is just for big kids," said Daniel.
Daniel and his friends paraded around the swings and the sandbox.
But everywhere they went, Margaret went too!

"Mom!" said Daniel. "I don't want Margaret to be in the parade. She's too little."

"Hmm," said Mom, "I wonder if we can make room for everyone in the parade, even little tigers?"

"That would be different," said Daniel.

"It will be different, but *when a baby makes things different, find a way to make things fun,*" Mom reminded Daniel.

Daniel looked over at Margaret, and she made a silly face. Daniel giggled. "Margaret, you are so silly!" Just then Daniel got another grr-ific idea!

"Maybe . . . Margaret can be the clown in our parade. That would be different and fun," said Daniel.

"Booboobooboo," said Margaret.

"Let the parade begin . . . again!" said Daniel happily. And they all paraded around the playground together.

"I loved playing at the playground today with Margaret," said Daniel. "Do you have a baby in your family? How do you feel when things are different? It's different for me with Baby Margaret. But now I know that different can be fun! Ugga Mugga!"